The Boxcar Children Mysteries

THE MYSTERY OF
THE TRAVELING TOMATOES

created by
GERTRUDE CHANDLER WARNER

Illustrated by Robert Papp

ALBERT WHITMAN & Company
Morton Grove, Illinois

The Mystery of the Traveling Tomatoes
Created by Gertrude Chandler Warner;
Illustrated by Robert Papp.

ISBN: 978-0-8075-5579-8 (hardcover)
ISBN: 978-0-8075-5580-4 (paperback)

For information about Albert Whitman & Company,
visit our web site at www.albertwhitman.com.

Contents

THE MYSTERY OF THE
TRAVELING TOMATOES

CHAPTER 1

The Traveling Tomatoes

"My tomatoes are moving!" Six-year-old Benny Alden stood in the garden. He squinted one eye and looked down a row of tomato plants. Yesterday, the row was nice and neat. Today the rows looked zig-zagged.

Benny's brother and two sisters gardened nearby. The Alden children were helping grow vegetables behind the Applewood Café, one of their very favorite restaurants.

"Plants don't just get up and walk around," said his sister Jessie.

"These did," said Benny.

Fourteen-year-old Henry walked over and stood behind Benny. The two brothers peered down the row of tomatoes. "They do look cockeyed," said Henry. "Have you measured them?"

"Not yet," said Benny. He opened the "Measuring Workbook" Henry had made to teach him how to measure things. Benny learned how to use a scale to measure how much things weighed. Here in the garden, he used a ruler to measure how far apart he planted the plants. "I planted the tomatoes two rulers, or twenty-four inches apart," he said. "But look." He moved the ruler this way and that between the plants. They measured ten inches apart, or thirty-six inches, all sorts of odd numbers.

Jessie pulled weeds nearby. The twelve-year-old still did not believe plants could move around all by themselves. "Maybe animals dug around your plants," she said. "It might have been raccoons, or dogs, or rabbits."

"Jessie's . . . probably . . . right," huffed

ten-year-old Violet. She tugged and lugged a small wagon through the soft garden soil. The wagon was piled high with stacks of old newspapers. "Remember, last week your . . . turnips were all . . . jumbled up?" she said. "That's why we made Spooky."

Spooky the Scarecrow smiled down at them. He wore the faded shirt and old pair of pants Grandfather had donated to the garden. The children had stuffed the clothing with straw. They made Spooky's head out of a muddy green bag they'd found in the alley behind the café. Benny used Violet's markers to draw a smiley face. Jessie stuffed the bag with straw and Violet sewed the head to Spooky's body. When the scarecrow was ready, Henry nailed Spooky to a large post in the middle of the garden. Spooky was supposed to keep critters from eating the food in their garden.

Benny looked at Spooky, then looked at his messy tomato plants. "You're not scaring anything," he said. "I should have given you a scarier face."

Jessie and Violet lifted the newspapers off the wagon. They spread them on the ground around the plants. The newspapers would keep weeds from growing.

After a little while, Violet noticed that her sister had stopped working. "Are you all right?" she asked.

Jessie perched on her hands and knees, peering down at a page of the *Greenfield Gazette*. "Listen to this," she said. " 'Baffling Bank Robbery. It's been two months since a thief disguised as an armored car driver robbed the Greenfield Bank. The robber looked like—' "

Applewood Café's back door banged open. "Time for lunch," called Laura Shea, the café's owner. She balanced a chubby baby on each hip. She smiled at the young gardeners. "Anyone hungry?" The Aldens didn't need to be called twice. They quickly ran inside to wash up.

There were many things the children loved about the small café. Henry, who was very good at building things, liked the old saws, hammers, and other tools hanging everywhere around the room. Benny liked the café's "Then and Now" photos. In one old "then" photo, Greenfield farmers drove horses and carts along Main Street to carry their vegetables to market. The "now" photo showed the same street filled with cars and shops. Benny especially liked the photos showing the café the day the Sheas bought it. Laura and David Shea stood smiling in front of a rickety old house. They smiled even though the porch was falling off and the roof was falling in. Prickly weeds grew all around, and the windows were boarded up with big sheets of metal. A faded red, white, and blue sign that read "For Sale by Sally" stood in front.

Violet, who liked things clean and tidy, liked the "now" photo better. The Sheas had painted the old house powder blue. They'd put on a new roof and porch. Large windows replaced the sheets of metal. The weedy back yard became a beautiful garden. The ugly old house changed into a bright, cozy restaurant.

The Sheas grew much of the food they served at the café. But then last year, Mrs. Shea had twins! After Sophie and Tatum were born, she was worried that she would be too busy with the babies and the café to plant the vegetables. The Aldens volunteered to help out in the garden. They enjoyed hard work, and they were happy to lend a hand where they could.

The Aldens learned plenty of new things while working in the garden. The secret to the Applewood Café garden was something the Sheas called "Black Gold." One day Mrs. Shea showed the Aldens three big cans full of rich black soil called compost.

"Rumpelstiltskin spun gold out of straw," she'd told them. "David and I spin gold out of garbage." She had picked up a fat worm and held it in her palm. "At the end of each day, we toss our kitchen and garden scraps into these cans. Hundreds of red wrigglers live inside. We feed the worms free meals, and they turn the garbage into gold." As the worm moved, it left behind something that looked like a small piece of pencil lead.

"Is that . . . worm poop?" asked Benny. Mrs. Shea laughed. "It's called a casting. But, yes, Benny, it *is* worm poop. And it's this 'black gold' that makes our plants grow so big and strong."

The Aldens had been amazed that something so small could make such a big difference.

Now their lunch was ready at the café. "Here you go," said Mrs. Shea, setting the plates on the table. Benny and Henry ate the Hopple-Popple, which was eggs scrambled with pieces of hot dogs, potatoes, and onions. Violet's tuna salad was mixed with grapes and raisins and served inside a scooped-out tomato picked fresh from the garden. Jessie ordered the fresh fruit plate that came with a cup of strawberry yogurt and slice of banana bread.

As the hungry gardeners dug into their delicious meals, other customers arrived for lunch. A sour-faced woman walked in with a husky young man. She plucked a menu from the counter and bent her nose to the page.

"Who can read such small print?" she complained. "And what are *those?*" She pointed at pretty little plants decorating the tables. "Is that parsley?" she said. "Mint? Basil?" She sniffed. "Whoever heard of putting herbs on tables instead of flowers? Humph!"

"Come on, Aunt Faye." The man led her into the café. "Let's find a table."

As they passed the Aldens, the woman peered at everyone's food. "What is that supposed to be?" she asked.

"Oh," said Jessie, "this is—"

But the woman wasn't listening. She frowned at the children's clothing. "Hasn't anyone taught you how to dress for a restaurant?" She glowered at Violet's braids. Violet had clipped them up on top of her head to keep them from dragging in the garden dirt. "Such an odd hairstyle," said the woman.

"Let's *go*, Aunt Faye." The burly man led his aunt to a table. "I told you we should have gone to *Le Grand Paris.* You won't find noisy children dining at fine French restaurants."

Benny glanced at his brother and sisters. "Were we being noisy?" he whispered.

"We were not," Violet whispered back.

A man wearing a vest with many pockets sat at the table behind the Aldens. He leaned a metal detector against the wall. The children often saw people using detectors in the park and at the beach. They knew that the detectors found coins, jewelry, and other metal objects people lost.

Mr. Shea, who was the café's chef, came out of the kitchen to the Aldens' table. "How's my fantastic four?" he said, his voice booming. He slid a dish of fresh-baked cookies on the table. Then he set down a piece of paper and a pen. "Here's your puzzle for the day," he said. "Have fun."

The children bent over the paper. Every time they came in, Mr. Shea gave them a new photo puzzle to solve. "Find Ten Differences," it said at the top of the page. Below were two photos of a park. At first, the photos looked exactly alike. But as the children searched, they found differences.

"This photo has four shovels in the sandbox," said Benny. "The other has five." Henry circled the shovels with a pen.

Jessie pointed to the bike. "This has a bell on the handlebars," she said. "The other has a toy Tyrannosaurus Rex."

The children circled seven more differences but they couldn't find the tenth. "We'll look at this later," said Henry. "We should get back to work." Henry and the girls stood but Benny kept studying the two pictures. "Benny?" said Henry.

Benny didn't hear him. He stared at the photos so hard his eyeballs hurt. "There!" he cried, jabbing the photo with his finger. "There!"

"Where?" said the others.

Benny pointed to a small cloud in the corner of each picture. "This one is shaped like a bear, but this one is shaped like a dog."

"High-five!" cried the others, slapping Benny's hands. Benny may have been the youngest, but everyone agreed he was the

Puzzle King of the Alden family.

When the children were done with lunch, they picked up their dishes to bring to the kitchen. "Henry," said Benny, "when we get back to the garden, can I shovel some of our black gold around my onions?" The man with the metal detector leaned back in his chair, listening with interest.

"Good idea," said Henry.

"Laura said there's *hundreds* in the garbage cans," said Jessie. The man tilted his chair so far back he nearly fell over.

The children passed the table with the sour-faced woman. Her nephew chewed a hamburger with his mouth open. Bits of bun, ketchup, and burger dotted his shirt. He shoved a small hot pepper into his mouth. The woman stopped the Aldens. "You children," she said, "are not properly dressed for such a nice restaurant."

"We are helping in the garden," explained Violet. The children always brushed the dirt off their clothes and scrubbed their hands well before eating.

"Still," said the woman, "it is important to dress nicely at all times." She nodded toward her nephew who slurped a milkshake. "My nephew, Fenster used to be quite sloppy. When he first came to visit, I constantly looked through his drawers and closet, mending this, washing that. Thanks to my help, he now dresses well, and he traded his awful old truck for a lovely new car. Now he has a most important job." She patted Fenster's hand. "He volunteers with the Greenfield Special Events Committee." Fenster rolled his eyes and made a face as he popped another hot pepper in his mouth. His aunt smiled. "It is so very important to make a good impression on people."

The Alden children were too polite to say that it is what is *inside* a person that matters. What the children *did* notice was a grown-up man who had never learned to chew with his mouth closed.

The children went on towards the kitchen. "When will we be able to dig up some of our buried treasure?" asked Violet.

Fenster choked. He started coughing and

gasping. "Slowly, dear," chided his aunt, "we must chew, chew, chew slowly." He grabbed his milkshake, gulping big swigs, making a huge milkshake moustache. Benny tried not to giggle.

Back in the garden, the children set to work. Their giant sunflowers towered over them. The bright yellow heads, heavy with sunflower seeds, were starting to bend. "We need to tie them to tall sticks," said Jessie, "so they don't plop over."

Benny plucked a cherry tomato from a vine and popped it into his mouth. It tasted warm and minty. Some overripe tomatoes lay splattered on the garden soil.

Henry put rocks on the sheets of newspaper his sisters had placed to keep the weeds from growing. The rocks would hold the newspaper down. He looked at the bank robbery article Jessie had started reading.

"What a strange story," Henry said. "The bank was robbed while we were away on vacation." He picked up the paper and read aloud:

BAFFLING BANK ROBBERY

It has been two months since a thief disguised as an armored car driver robbed the Greenfield Bank.

"The robber looked like Noah, our regular driver," said bank president Arlo Judge. "He came at 12:20, Noah's regular time. And he was driving the sort of silver armored car Noah drives. We handed him our moneybags, just like we always do. We didn't know we'd been robbed until an hour later when our real driver pulled up in the real armored car. By that time, the thief had escaped with the money."

Police have not found the fake armored car, the thief, or the money. No witnesses have come forward. There are still no clues to the robbery. Anyone with information should contact the Greenfield Police.

"I would have noticed a silver armored truck," said Benny, who could name almost every kind of car and truck.

"Someone must have seen *something*," said Jessie. "I can't believe there aren't any clues."

"Yikes!" Benny's feet flew out from under

him and he landed with a thud. "I'm okay, " he said, scrambling up. "I just slipped on a tomato!"

Violet thought about the article, too. "Why was the armored car driver an hour late picking up the bank's money?" she asked.

"This article doesn't give enough information," said Henry. "We'd probably need to go back and read the newspaper stories that were written right after the robbery. Maybe we should. I know I'd like to know what happened. "

"Me, too. We can look up the articles at the library," said Jessie. "They keep all the issues of the *Greenfield Gazette.*"

"Let's find out more!" said Benny. "It's just like a mystery." He thought for a moment. "It *is* a mystery."

It was decided. The Aldens would go to the library the next day and learn all they could about the great Greenfield Bank robbery.

CHAPTER 2

The Bank Robbery

"You want to know more about the bank robbery?" asked Ms. Connelly, the head librarian.

"Yes," said Henry. "We'd like to read articles written the first few days after the robbery."

"Back in a jiffy," she said as she went into a room behind the front desk. It was well known around Greenfield that the Alden children loved a good mystery. They often used the library to track down clues.

Moments later, Ms. Connelly returned with an armload of newspapers. "These came out the week of the robbery," she said. "Let me know if you need more."

The children spread out on the carpet in the children's reading corner. Each of them took a newspaper to read. "BRAZEN BANK ROBBERY," read the headline of Violet's paper.

"This article says the silver armored car pulled up to the bank at its usual time," Violet said as she read. "The driver walked in, gave his usual greeting, picked up the bags of money, and left. An hour later, the *real* driver walked in."

Jessie held up her newspaper. "Here's a photo of the real driver," she said. A large man stared at the camera. He had a bushy black moustache. Long black sideburns stuck out of his driver's cap. He wore big sunglasses. The label under the photo said "Noah Gabriel, armored car driver."

While the other children searched the newspapers for articles, Benny looked at the news photos. Although the six-year-old could read many words, most newspaper stories still seemed hard to understand. Suddenly, he saw words he understood very well. "The circus comes to town," he read aloud.

"Benny, that was great!" said Jessie. "Can you read more?" They all listened as Benny sounded out the story about the Spectacular Shayna Circus arriving in Greenfield.

One photo in the paper showed animals, clowns, and performers arriving in colorful circus railroad cars.

"Our boxcar doesn't look anything like these," said Benny.

It was true. The Aldens' boxcar wasn't nearly as fancy. They'd discovered it when they had been alone in the world. After their parents died, they ran away to live on their own. They feared they would be found and sent to live with their grandfather, who they had never met. They thought he might be mean to them. The children found shelter in an old railroad car in the woods. It quickly became their home, and they lived there happily until Grandfather found them. When the children saw how nice he was and how much he loved them, they went to live with him in Greenfield. Later, as a surprise, Grandfather had their boxcar brought to their backyard so they could play in it any time they liked.

Benny looked at the picture of the circus train. He turned to Violet, who was a wonderful artist. "Maybe you could paint our boxcar to look like these circus train cars. Maybe you could—"

"Look!" Henry pointed at the date on Benny's newspaper. "The circus came to town the same day the bank was robbed!" He opened Benny's newspaper to a special circus section. In one, five people in bright yellow shirts stood under a sign that said, *Greenfield Special Events Committee welcomes the Spectacular Shayna Circus.* Four of the people greeted the circus ringmaster. The fifth person stood smiling and waving at the reporter's camera. It was a young man.

"That's the man at the Applewood Café," said Benny. "The one who said we were noisy."

Jessie nodded. "The one who chewed with his mouth open."

"His name is Fenster," said Violet, remembering. "His aunt said he volunteers on the Special Events Committee. It sure looks like a fun job."

"There's Chief Morgan," said Benny. The photo showed the chief of police keeping the crowds on the sidewalk. Behind him, a line of elephants led the circus parade down Main Street. "The March of the Elephants," said the caption. Behind the elephants, the hands of the giant city hall clock pointed straight up.

"This picture was taken at noon," said Violet. "The newspaper articles say the bank was robbed at twenty minutes after noon."

Henry tugged his bottom lip, thinking.

"What if the circus and the bank robbery are connected?"

"How?" asked Jessie.

"What if the robber *knew* the whole town would be on Main Street watching the circus parade? That would be a great time to rob a bank."

The last photo showed circus workers setting up big tents in Pleasant Valley Park. In the background, the people in yellow shirts helped Police Chief Morgan put up ropes to hold back the crowd.

"We should ask Chief Morgan about the robbery," said Henry. "He always remembers everything."

Benny laughed. "Just like an elephant."

* * * *

Chief Morgan was the Aldens' friend and every Saturday he played chess in the park. The next day, the children biked along the path, coasting around the playground. As they rode, they noticed the man with a metal detector searching under the monkey bars. Jessie remembered that he had been at the café the day before.

At last, the Aldens found Chief Morgan

at one of the cement chess tables. He played chess with an elderly man.

"Checkmate!" whooped the man. The chief laughed. "Good game, Cesar." Then he saw the children ride up. "Cesar, I'd like you to meet the Aldens. Their grandfather, James Alden, is one of my oldest friends. Children, this is Cesar Canton."

One by one, each child shook the older man's hand. "Pleased to meet you," they each said in turn.

"Likewise," said Cesar. The two men began setting up their chess pieces for the next game.

"We were wondering," Henry said to Chief Morgan, "if you can tell us about the bank robbery. We can wait until you finish your game."

"Go ahead and talk," said Cesar, standing. "These old legs of mine would enjoy a nice stroll around the park." Leaning on his cane, he walked off toward the rose garden.

The children gathered around Chief Morgan. "You know," he said, "I can't help feeling that

the bank robbery was a little bit my fault."

"*Your* fault?" said Henry.

The chief sighed. "The armored car driver, Noah Gabriel, is a friend of mine. It's because of me he was late picking up the money from the bank."

"What happened?" asked Violet.

"Well, Noah always keeps exactly the same schedule," said Chief Morgan. "Every day at noon, he picks up the bank's money. Then he drives the money to the AAA Armored Car Company vault. Then he goes to lunch."

"But he didn't do that the day of the robbery," said Jessie.

"Right, that was my fault," said Chief Morgan. "The Events Committee asked the police to close Main Street for the circus parade. I knew Noah had to drive across Main Street on his way to and from the bank. I didn't want my friend to have to sit and wait in his armored car for an hour until the parade passed by."

"It's boring to sit and wait in a car," agreed Benny.

The chief sighed. "So, I called Noah. I told him he should eat lunch before he picked up the money from the bank. That way, by the time he finished eating, the parade would have passed by. Then Noah could drive across Main Street without having to wait." Chief Morgan looked sadder than ever. "I was just trying to do a good deed. Instead, I gave the thief enough time to rob the bank and make his getaway."

Cesar returned from his walk. "It's great to be outdoors," he said, setting his cane next to the chessboard. "I can't stand being cooped up in my daughter's apartment all day."

"Cesar was a farmer," explained the chief. "But farming is hard work. A few months ago, Cesar's daughter had him sell the farm and move in with her."

"Now I live fifteen stories up in the sky," said Cesar, waving his cane in the air. "You can't grow anything in the sky. The old farmer winked at the children. "The sky is for the birds. Humans should live near the soil."

"I love dirt!" said Benny.

"We help in the Applewood Café's garden," Jessie explained. "We grow tomatoes and cucumbers and watermelons and potatoes and—"

Cesar's eyes twinkled. "It's good that you like growing things."

"Come help us," said Violet. "There's always plenty of work to do."

Cesar shook his head. "My daughter won't let me garden anymore," he said. "She worries the work is too hard. But I thank you for asking." He turned to the chief. "Would you like another chance to try to beat me?"

"You bet," said Chief Morgan.

The children biked to the playground and stopped to swing. "Chief Morgan looked so sad," said Violet. "It's awful that he thinks the robbery was even the tiniest little bit his fault."

"Maybe we can figure out who robbed the bank," said Benny. "That would cheer him up."

Jessie leaned far back, pumping her legs, swinging as high as she could. "What if the thief was someone from the circus?" she called to the others. "Just like Henry said. While everyone watched the March of the Elephants, he could have robbed the bank, then slipped back into the parade. No one would have noticed."

"And the circus left town a week later," said Violet. "That could explain why the thief and the money were never found."

"But it doesn't explain the armored truck," said Henry. "It's easy enough to hide stolen money on a circus train. But where could he hide an armored truck?"

They pumped their swings higher and higher. They watched as the man with the metal detector moved to the soccer field. He wore big headphones, listening as he swung the long metal wand back and forth along the ground.

"That looks like fun," said Benny.

"They sell that same metal detector at Hamu's Hardware," Henry said. "Maybe Mr. Hamu will let us try it."

The children slowed their swings and jumped off.

"And while we're on Main Street," Jessie said, "we can ask the shop owners if they remember anything about the day of the bank robbery."

CHAPTER 3

Invisible Airplanes

Henry led the way through the aisles of Hamu's Hardware. It was his favorite place to buy nails, tools, paint, and other building supplies. He knew where to find everything. "Here they are," he said, stopping in front of a display of metal detectors.

A gray-haired man with twinkling eyes came over. "And what are the Aldens building today?" asked Mr. Hamu.

"Benny wants to try that metal detector," said Henry, pointing to one.

Mr. Hamu lifted it off the shelf. "Model X332," he said. "The best one made. *Very* expensive. I only sell one or two a year." He put the headphones on Benny's ears. He showed Benny how to swing the detector slowly back and forth over the ground. Then he took coins out of his pocket and rolled them down the aisle.

Benny moved the detector toward a coin. "I hear clicks," he said. He moved closer. "The clicks are getting faster." He moved the detector right over the coin. "It's buzzing!"

While Benny hunted down the coins, the others asked Mr. Hamu what he remembered about the day of the bank robbery.

"I remember the circus parade," Mr. Hamu said. "All our customers went outside to watch. So we closed up shop and watched it, too. We didn't hear about the bank robbery until later."

Benny brought the detector back. "Thank you for letting me try this," he told Mr. Hamu. Then the Aldens said good-bye and left.

"Let's go talk to the other shop owners about the robbery," said Violet. "Maybe we'll find a clue."

The children went next door to Cora's Costumes. The owner, Cora, was helping a customer try on a king's costume. Cora was dressed like Little Bo Peep. She also wore a curly clown wig that was all the colors of the rainbow.

"May I help you?" asked Cora.

"We're wondering what you remember about the day of the bank robbery," said Henry.

"Oh, my dears, we were much too busy that day to notice anything." She handed the king his crown. "The circus was in town, so people were throwing circus parties. We were mobbed by people renting costumes—clowns, animals, fire-eaters, lion tamers—simply mobbed."

The children's luck was no better as they walked in and out of all the shops up one side of Main Street and down the other. None of the storekeepers or customers remembered anything about the robbery. All anyone remembered was the circus parade.

The children's last stop was Witlin's Watch Works. They parked their bikes in front of a tangle of tomato plants. Instead of nice neat rows, the plants grew wild in the soil outside the shop. Overripe tomatoes had fallen from the vines and splattered on the ground. "Be careful," warned Benny. He was still sore from slipping on the tomatoes in the garden. "Those things are *dangerous.*"

Inside the watch shop, the sour-faced woman and her nephew Fenster stood at the counter. Fenster held up a wide watchband that had two small watches on it. "I like this," he said. "See, I can set each watch to a different time." He turned the watch stems. "There, I set the top watch on Greenfield time and the bottom watch for Paris."

"Why Paris?" asked his aunt.

"It's just an example," snapped Fenster. "I was mentioning a place that has a different time than here. Right now, it's six hours later in Paris."

"You already have twelve watches in your top dresser drawer," said his aunt.

Fenster scowled. "Why are you always going through my things?"

"*Someone* has to straighten properly," the aunt said. She noticed the Aldens. "I see you children have cleaned up nicely," she said, plucking a speck of dust from Jessie's sleeve.

Fenster tried on the watch and frowned.

"This band is too tight," he said.

"I can fix it for you in a week," said Mr. Witlin.

"That's too late," said Fenster. "I need it Tuesday."

"All right." Mr. Witlin measured Fenster's wrist. "The watch will be ready at three o'clock Tuesday."

Fenster took out a fat roll of bills and counted out the money for the watch. "Tuesday, three o'clock," he said, turning abruptly, nearly bumping into the children. He gripped his aunt's arm. "Come on," he said, rushing her out the door, "I have to get to work."

The children asked Mr. Witlin what he

remembered about the day of the robbery. But, like everyone else, he was watching the parade while the bank was being robbed.

Back outside, Jessie said, "It really does seem like the thief planned the robbery to take place during the parade."

"We haven't asked in that shop," said Benny, leading the way to the ice cream shop next door.

But the owner was no help. "Those elephants were huge," he said. "And those clowns were so funny . . . " He only remembered the circus as well.

The Aldens wondered what to do next. Benny pressed his nose against the glass display window. "As long as we're here, we could have some ice cream!" he said.

The children gave their orders. Benny had vanilla in a cone. Jessie ordered strawberry and vanilla. Violet decided to try the rainbow sherbet, and Henry had a taste for rocky road. Then they sat at one of the tables outside the shop to enjoy their treats. A woman at the next table fed ice cream to her toddler.

Benny finished his cone before it could melt. "We'll never solve the robbery case," he said, popping the pointy bottom of the cone into his mouth. "No one saw anything."

"We can't give up," said Violet. "We've just begun."

Henry borrowed Jessie's notebook and took out a pen. "All right," he said, "what are some things we know about the day of the robbery?"

As Jessie, Violet, and Benny recalled what they'd learned, Henry wrote it all down. Soon he had a list of facts:

- *The March of the Elephants led the circus down Main Street at noon.*
- *The bank was robbed at 12:20.*
- *The thief dressed like an armored car driver.*
- *The thief disguised himself to look like the driver, Noah:*
  - *He wore a bushy moustache.*
  - *He wore big dark sunglasses.*
  - *He drove a silver van that looked like Noah's armored car.*

Then the children thought of other things that *might* be true:

- *Noah was a big man, so the thief was probably a big man.*

"He could have walked on stilts to look taller," said Benny. He thought of Spooky the Scarecrow. "And maybe he stuffed straw in his clothes to look bigger."

"That's an interesting idea," said Jessie. "But I think people in the bank would notice a stilt-walking straw-padded man."

Henry nodded. "Let's try to think of some other things that might be true about the thief." He wrote them down:

- *The thief might live in Greenfield because:*
  - *He knew what the driver looked like because he disguised himself to look like Noah.*
  - *He knew that Noah always greeted the bank guard the same way.*
  - *He knew what time the driver always made his pick-up.*

Finally, Henry wrote down a list of questions:

- *How did the robber know that Noah would be late that day?*
- *Where did the thief get an armored car? Did he steal it?*
- *Where did the robber hide his armored car until he was ready to rob the bank?*
- *Where did he drive it after he robbed the bank?*
- *Why didn't anyone remember seeing the fake armored car?*

It was quiet for a moment as Henry finished writing the list.

"Pay-pay! Pay-pay!" squealed the toddler at the table next to them. "Pay-pay!" he yelled, laughing, pointing at the sky. The Aldens looked up. A jet plane flew high overhead. They could barely hear it.

"He always hears the airplanes," his mother said.

"That's amazing," said Violet.

The mother smiled. "Actually, we all hear the airplanes. But as we grow up, we get used to the sound and we stop paying attention. Airplanes are new for babies, so they notice. But, for us, it's as if the airplanes are invisible."

"Birdy, birdy," squealed the toddler, pointing to a nearby tree. Sure enough, two birds sat chirping on a branch. Again, the children hadn't even noticed the birds before.

As the Aldens rode their bikes home, Henry braked to a sudden stop. "I think I know why no one saw the robber's armored car the day of the robbery. It was as invisible to them as that airplane and the birds were to us."

"How can a big silver truck be invisible?" asked Benny.

"It wasn't *really* invisible," Henry explained. "But people are so used to seeing that same truck on that same street at that same time, they don't pay attention."

* * * *

The children rode their bikes through the park. Workers in yellow shirts set up tents for Sunday's 5K Healthy Heart run. The whole Alden family had signed up. Henry, a very good runner, would run the 5K, which was a little over three miles. Jessie, who had been practicing running each day, was going to try it, too. Violet and Benny signed up to walk with the One Milers. Their housekeeper, Mrs. McGregor, Grandfather, and their dog, Watch would join the Simply Strollers. They would walk around the park until the runners returned.

"Look," said Benny pointing across the park. The man with the metal detector crouched under the baseball bleachers. He dug around in the dirt with a small shovel. Then he picked up a small object, brushed it off, and tucked it into a vest pocket. "I wonder what he found," Benny said.

Next, the Aldens stopped at the fountain for a drink. Nearby, all the Greenfield Special Events Committee members were working hard, except Fenster. He leaned against a tree, eating a candy bar. "Pull that tent rope tighter," he shouted. "No, no, the other rope. And, you over there . . . "

"Fenster and his aunt sure are bossy," said Benny.

"There is a nice way and a rude way to ask someone to do something," said Jessie, who did not like Fenster's way at all. "You can catch more flies with honey than with vinegar," Mrs. McGregor liked to say. Although Jessie never understood why anyone would want to catch flies at all.

Violet always tried to find something nice to say about a person. "One good thing about Fenster," she said, "is that his committee does put on wonderful events. They brought the circus to town, and now they're putting on the race."

But even as she said this, Fenster crumpled his candy wrapper and tossed it on the ground. Then he walked toward a tent, yelling instructions.

Without a word, Violet rode over, picked up the red wrapper, and tossed it into a garbage can. Few things made Violet angry. But littering was one of them.

At dinner that night, the children told Grandfather about their search for clues to the robbery.

"No one saw the armored car," Henry said. "At least they don't remember seeing it. But maybe they were so used to it that they just didn't notice."

"Like airplanes," said Benny, "and birds."

Jessie told Grandfather about the toddler who noticed everything. "But is it possible to find something that's invisible?" she asked.

Grandfather thought this over. "Yes, I think you sometimes can. For example, you can't see the wind. But you find it every time you fly a kite or hear leaves rustling on the trees."

Henry twirled his fork in his plate of spaghetti. "Maybe instead of looking for the robber's armored truck, the police should have looked for a place big enough to hide it," he said.

"We can do that," said Jessie. She took a piece of hot garlic bread and passed the plate around. "We can go to the bank, then follow the same route the armored car usually followed." She scrunched her mouth. "Except we don't know the route."

"I happen to know the woman who owns the AAA Armored Car Company," said Grandfather. "Maybe she can help you."

"That's a great idea," said Jessie. "We can talk to her on Monday."

The next morning was Sunday, the day of the Healthy Heart Race. There were hundreds of people in the park getting ready to run 5K, walk a mile, or just walk around the park. Henry and Jessie proudly pinned their running numbers onto their shirts.

The Sheas jogged up. Mr. Shea pushed the twins in a double stroller. "We closed the café so we could run, too," he said.

Jessie retied her running shoes. "I'm not sure I'll be able to run three whole miles."

"Then run with us," said Mrs. Shea. "We won't be going too fast with the twins. Besides, we're running just for the fun of it. We won't mind stopping to walk a while."

The race began. The 5K runners ran one lap around the park then sped off to circle through town. Meanwhile, Benny and Violet walked a mile, which was twice around the

park. When they finished, they ate bananas that had been set out for the runners.

A roar went up as the first 5K runners returned to the park. People waiting at the finish line waved big posters, cheering as friends and family crossed the finish line. The Aldens quickly joined the waiting crowd, yelling proudly as Henry came in. He was, they all agreed, very fast for a fourteen-year-old.

Jessie and the Sheas jogged in a few minutes later.

"I did it!" said Jessie, her cheeks bright red. "I ran all the way and didn't stop even one time."

CHAPTER 4

Worms!

Early Monday before breakfast, the children rode their bikes through the quiet morning streets. As usual, Benny pedaled extra hard, leading all the way to the Applewood Café. He coasted around to the garden.

"Oh, no!" He screeched to a stop. "Our black gold!"

Three huge garbage cans lay on their sides. Their lids were torn off and their insides spilled out. Scattered on the ground around them were wilted lettuce leaves and broccoli stems, watermelon rinds and dead flowers, grass clippings, and mounds of black dirt. The dirt looked like it was moving. It *was* moving. Hundreds of worms squiggled around.

"Quick," shouted Henry, grabbing a shovel, "before they get away!"

Jessie picked up the cans. Henry shoveled wormy dirt into each one. Violet pulled on her gardening gloves and scooped up the food scraps, tossing them into the cans. Benny raced around, picking up all the wiggly worms he could find. He set them gently into the cans.

Now the four children finished cleaning up the spilled cans. "Raccoons must have done this," Jessie said.

Violet studied the latches on the cans. "I don't think raccoons could open these."

"And I don't think raccoons wear boots." Benny pointed to footprints. The deep boot treads made a *V* shaped pattern. One *V* had no point on the bottom. The children followed the prints from the garbage cans,

through the garden, and out into the alley. At first, the boot treads left a lot of dirt to track. But, as the dirt wore off, the trail became harder and harder to follow. After a block, the children could not see the prints.

"Why would someone dump our black gold?" asked Violet as they headed back. But no one could think of a single reason.

Benny spotted something shiny glinting in the tall weeds along Applewood's alley fence. He reached in and picked up a toy car. "Aw, all the wheels are missing," he said, tossing it into a garbage can. There were a few green cloth bags in the garbage, like the one he used to make Spooky's head. Maybe they should make another scarecrow. Spooky wasn't scaring anything.

"Come on, Benny," Henry said, running toward the old building next door. "Let's build up our buried treasure."

Tall stacks of tires leaned against the old building, which used to be Duffy's Garage. The boys lifted a few tires off the piles and rolled them to their garden. They'd set the tires on top of a circle of other old tires. Inside the circle, leafy potato vines grew out of black soil. Benny called the potatoes their "buried treasure" because the potatoes grew under the dirt. Every couple of weeks, as the plants grew taller, the boys added more tires and more soil.

Jessie knelt in the cucumber patch, hunting for ripe cucumbers that hid among the leaves. She noticed that the droopy sunflowers now stood nice and straight. Someone had tied them to tall bamboo sticks. "Did you prop up the sunflowers?" she asked her sister.

Violet looked surprised. "No," she said. "Mrs. Shea must have done that after yesterday's race."

"Hey!" said Benny. "Somebody moved my green peppers!" He measured a row of plants, then checked his measuring workbook. "I planted these peppers twelve inches apart. Now the plants are all messed up. Just like my tomato plants."

"Maybe the same person who tipped over our compost cans moved your peppers," said

Jessie. Benny checked the dirt for boot prints, but there were none. There also weren't any animal footprints—no raccoons or rabbits.

All he saw were regular old shoe prints, from regular old shoes.

"Here's something," said Henry, pointing to a dent in the soil. "I've seen these strange marks in the dirt all around the garden today."

Some of Spooky the Scarecrow's straw poked out of his shirt. Benny tucked it back inside. "Spooky," he said, "have you been messing with our garden?" But the green-faced scarecrow just looked down at Benny and smiled his crooked smile.

Mrs. Shea called them in for breakfast. Violet spooned mango and strawberry jam into the center of thin pancakes Mr. Shea called crepes. "Crepes rhymes with apes," he'd said. "But crepes taste better."

Violet rolled each crepe into a log and took bite after delicious bite. Benny filled his plate with scrambled eggs and fresh-baked whole wheat bread. Jessie cut a jumbo raisin muffin into slices, carefully spreading each slice with sweet butter. And Henry helped himself to second servings of everything.

As Mrs. Shea brought a pitcher of milk to the table, the children told her about the overturned compost cans. "I can't imagine who would do such mischief," she said. "There is nothing inside those cans of value."

"Except worm . . . er . . . black gold," said Benny. He figured it wasn't polite to say "worm poop" at the breakfast table.

As they finished eating, Mr. Shea came out of the kitchen with a platter of melon slices and strawberries. He set down a new picture puzzle and winked. "This one is super-duper hard."

The children studied two nearly identical photos of a soccer game. They worked for a long time but found only fourteen differences. Once again, Benny spotted the last and hardest clue. Two players' helmets had different colored chinstraps.

"Is it time to go to the armored car company yet?" Benny asked when they finished.

Henry glanced at his watch. "Yes," he said.

This time, Henry led the way as they rode their bikes across town.

CHAPTER 5

The Scene of the Crime

The children pressed the doorbell of the large gray building. *Whirrrrrr. Whirrrrrr.* The security camera over the door searched left, then right, then down until it found the children. The door buzzer sounded, and the children walked in.

A tall smiling lady with twinkling blue eyes and blond curly hair greeted them in the lobby. "Your grandfather told me you might stop by," she said. "I'm Edie Hope, the owner of the company. I'm on the phone just now.

I'll be back in a minute."

While they waited, the children looked at a large display called *A Half-Century of Service*. It showed photos of the different armored cars and uniforms used by the AAA Armored Car Company over the past fifty years. The children recognized the newest cars, which they often saw driving around town. These were silver with green lettering the color of money. The newest uniforms were dark blue with brass buttons.

The office door opened. "Sorry to keep you waiting," said Edie Hope. "Now, how can I help you?"

"We are interested in the robbery," Henry said.

Ms. Hope's smile faded. "This was our only robbery in fifty years. I can't believe the police still have no clues. "

"Where did the thief find an armored car?" asked Jessie. "Did he steal one from you?"

"No, we keep all our cars under lock and key."

Henry explained the children's idea. "If

you show us the route your armored car usually takes, maybe we can find where the thief hid the fake armored car."

Ms. Hope led them into her office. A giant street map of Greenfield covered one wall. She pointed to the top of the map. "The Greenfield Bank is all the way up here at the north end of Greenfield, and we are all the way down here at the south." Ms. Hope ran a finger straight down to the bottom. "Noah always drives straight up to the bank and back."

The children studied the map. A wide line ran across the middle. "It looks like Greenfield is wearing a belt," said Benny.

"That's Main Street." Henry pointed to the left side of the map. "Here, on the west, is the railroad station. The circus parade began here. "Then," he ran his finger to the right along Main Street, "the March of the Elephants led the parade east, all the way across town, to the park over here. Main Street was closed for an hour. No traffic was allowed to cross."

"Which means the robber was up here when the parade began—on the same side as the bank. He hid his armored car above Main Street until he was ready to rob the bank," said Jessie.

The children thanked Ms. Hope and headed out. "We'll start at the bank," said Henry, "and bike along Noah's route looking for a place big enough to hide an armored car."

"An invisible armored car," said Benny, who secretly wondered if they could find such a thing.

Next, the children went to the Greenfield Bank. Arlo Jeffries, the manager, knew the Aldens, who visited the bank every month to put part of their allowances into their savings accounts.

"We've come to ask about the robbery," said Henry. "What do you remember about that day?"

Mr. Jeffries sighed. "It was exactly like every other pick-up day. The armored car driver walked into the bank. We thought it was Noah. He was dressed in Noah's blue uniform. He had sunglasses. He had Noah's big moustache and long sideburns. Then Noah—I mean, the thief—walked to the teller's window, opened his duffle bag, loaded up the bags of cash, and left. Just like always. Except it wasn't Noah." He shook his head.

"Can you remember anything different that day?" asked Violet. "Even the smallest thing might be a clue."

Mr. Jeffries closed his eyes, thinking hard. "The circus, of course," he said. "The bank was nearly empty because our customers were watching the parade. Even my employees went there on their lunch break. The only ones here were the bank guard, the teller, and, of course, me."

Clink, clank, clank, clink! The children whirled around at the sound of clanking coins. The man with the metal detector had plunked down a green bag full of coins. "I want to trade these coins for paper money," the man told the teller. "Paper money is lighter to cart around." He spilled the coins onto the counter. A few fell to the floor and rolled away. The children helped pick them up. The man barely looked at the children as they returned the coins to the pile.

When Benny saw the coins, he remembered that the bank had a vending machine near the door. "Can we get candy?" he asked.

"We just ate breakfast," said Jessie.

"That was hours ago," Benny said.

"It was *one* hour," said Violet.

Mr. Jeffries snapped his fingers. "That reminds me! I must call the vending company right now. We've run out of Chili-Billy Bars." He bent down, whispering, "One of our customers gets angry if we run out. Though why someone wants to eat candy made with hot peppers is beyond me. I tried one once." He made a face and fanned his tongue with his hand. "Hot!" he said. "Hot and awful. *Awful.*"

* * * *

The children biked south, from the bank toward Main Street, looking for a place where someone could hide a big silver truck. They passed shops and parks, small houses without garages, a school, and a department store. A block from the Applewood Café, they passed a row of offices. A big red, white, and blue sign said: "Sales by Sally Realty."

"Look," said Henry, "that's the sign in the photo at the café. This is the lady who sold the café to the Sheas."

"There sure are a lot of places for sale," Jessie noticed. There were photos of houses, apartments, and shops taped up all over the big picture window of the office.

Benny pointed to a faded photo of Duffy's Garage. "Look, that's where we got those old tires," he said.

Below the photo were the words "GARAGE FOR SALE. MAKE AN OFFER." The children looked closely at the photo. Big sheets of metal covered the windows. Weeds grew in the gravel lot in back. A pile of old tires leaned against the back wall.

"I'll bet Sally knows every building in

Greenfield," said Jessie. "She might know where someone could hide a van. We should talk to her. But look—she's not here right now." A sign on Sally's door said "Back at 1:00."

Henry checked his watch. "That's three hours from now. Let's finish riding toward Main Street. We'll come back here after lunch."

The children followed the armored car route but, as hard as they tried, they couldn't find one single place where someone could hide a big armored car.

CHAPTER 6

Poison Ivy!

The Applewood Café bustled with lunchtime customers. As the Aldens waited for their orders, they discussed their visit to the armored car company and to the bank.

"The thief knew exactly how the real driver looked and talked," Henry said. "That means he'd been watching the real driver. The thief might live right here in Greenfield."

The smell of cooking food made Benny's stomach rumble. To pass the time until the food came, he looked at the old photo of the café hanging over their table. For the first time, he noticed Duffy's Garage in the background. The pile of old tires was higher back then. That was before Henry and Benny used them to build the planter for their potatoes. When Mr. Shea brought their food, Benny asked, "Does Duffy mind us using his old tires for our buried treasure?"

"We've never met Duffy," said Mrs. Shea. "But Sally, the lady who sold us the café, said he wouldn't mind. He moved away and just wants to sell the place." Benny poked his spoon through the crust of his chicken-pot-pie. He was so hungry he barely stopped to blow on each spoonful before putting it into his mouth.

"Slowly," said Violet, resting a gentle hand on Benny's shoulder, "Remember your manners."

Benny paused, his spoon halfway to his mouth. It was hard to eat slowly when he was so hungry! Slowly he ate the pie, tasting each pea and carrot and zucchini and onion he had helped plant and grow.

When they finished, Mr. Shea brought them each a warm peach cobbler topped with a scoop of vanilla ice cream. Then he pulled a new picture puzzle from his chef's apron. "This one is extra-super-hard," he said. "Good luck."

The children bent over the puzzle, looking for differences between the two photos of a toy store. "Benny," said Jessie, "what's wrong?"

Benny looked down. He didn't even realize he'd been scratching his wrist. But now he felt it itching. And his arm itched. "Your skin is all red," said Violet. "It's covered with blisters."

Now Benny couldn't stop scratching. His arm grew redder and redder. The children called Mrs. Shea, who took one look and said, "Poison ivy." She lopped off a piece of the aloe plant decorating their table. Thick gel oozed out and she dabbed it on Benny's arm. It felt cool and soothing.

"Remember this rhyme," said Mrs. Shea. "'Leaves of three, let them be.' Poison ivy

has three leaves. Benny, did you go into any woods, or deep weeds?"

Benny thought and thought. "I picked up a toy car in the alley this morning. It was in the weeds near the garbage cans."

"That could be it," said Mrs. Shea. "I'll go outside later and take a look." She brought Benny ice cubes wrapped in a towel. He kept them on the rash while he ate dessert and worked on the puzzle. By the time they finished lunch and headed out to Sally's Realty, both Benny's rash and his tummy were feeling much better.

* * * *

"An armored car, you say?" Sally was a large woman with short red hair and a hearty laugh. "You're looking for a place where someone could hide an armored car?"

The children nodded. They knew it was an odd question. "Well," Sally said, "an armored car is too tall to fit in a regular garage. But it might fit into some of the bigger garages being built behind new homes."

Henry shook his head. "A neighbor would notice an armored car pulling out of a garage. The person we're looking for couldn't risk being seen."

"Let's take a look." Sally clicked through photos on her computer. "Oh, would you look at this." She scrolled through photos of the broken-down shop that was now the Applewood Café. "The Sheas have worked miracles with that place," she said. "I sure hope someone buys Duffy's Garage next door and fixes that up, too."

"What happened to Duffy?" asked Jessie.

"A year ago, he packed up his things, said he was done fixing cars and moved to Florida. He told me to sell the place." She clicked to a screen filled with photos of Duffy's Garage. "Look at this mess. Duffy left old junk cars out back. No wonder no one wants to buy the place. In one year I've only had one person who was interested."

"Who was that?" asked Henry.

"A stranger stopped in a couple of months ago. He was a big man, as tall as my hubby

Harry. But he had long blond hair pulled back in a ponytail. He asked if he could rent the garage to work on his car. I called Mr. Duffy and he said it was OK. We were hoping the man might like the place enough to buy it," Sally said.

"Why didn't he?" asked Jessie.

"I guess he just left town. One morning I came to work and found the keys to Duffy's slipped under my door. When I went to check on the garage, it was all boarded up, just the way Duffy left it," Sally replied.

Violet looked at the photos. "What happened to all these old cars in the back of the garage?"

"Well, I couldn't sell the garage with that mess out back, so last month, I called Sam's Scrap Yard. Sam hauled everything but the tires," said Sally.

The Aldens thanked Sally for talking to them.

"You're welcome," said Sally. "And could you do me a favor?" She handed Jessie some photos. "Please give these to the Sheas for me." There were couple of old photos of the Applewood Café, before the Sheas bought it. There was also a batch of For Sale photos of Duffy's Garage. "Mrs. Shea said she'd put these up in the café," Sally said.

"That's a good idea," said Jessie. "Maybe a customer will see them and want to buy the garage."

Sally handed Jessie a key to Duffy's Garage as well. "Give this to Mrs. Shea, too. The key opens the side door. I told her to just go in and show the garage to anyone who wants a look."

*   *   *   *

"Benny Alden!" cried Mrs. McGregor. The Alden's housekeeper stared at the bright red splotches on Benny's arms. "It's poison ivy, indeed. You go upstairs this minute and soak in a cool bath." She checked the other children but only Benny had splotches. "And it's a bath for you, too," she told Watch, leading the dog to the laundry sink.

Poor Watch did not like baths. But Mrs. McGregor said he needed one.

"I'll wash Watch, because he might have rubbed against the poison ivy," she explained to Jessie. "His fur would protect him from a rash, but the poison could rub off on anyone who petted him."

At bedtime, the children gathered in Benny's room. Violet dipped the tips of cotton swabs into a bottle of pink Calamine lotion. Then she painted funny pink animals on Benny's rash to soothe the itching.

"This sure has been a busy day," said Jessie, yawning. "This morning we found our 'black gold' tipped over and had to round up our worms. Then we followed the boot prints of the person who did it out into the alley."

"And I found a toy car in the poison ivy," said Benny. "And someone moved my green pepper plants."

Violet finished drawing a pink giraffe on Benny's arm. "And, at the armored car office, Edie Hope showed us the route the armored car usually takes."

"And we went to the bank," said Benny, who really wished he'd brought money to buy a candy bar.

"Then we biked along the armored car route," said Henry, "from the bank all the way down to Main Street without seeing one place the crook could hide an armored car. And we talked to Sally at the real estate office."

Jessie brushed her hair. "I don't know about the rest of you, but between running the 5K yesterday, and riding my bike today, my legs ache."

"My whole self aches," said Benny, flopping back on his pillows. The children said goodnight and went to their rooms.

Benny couldn't sleep. Part of the problem was the itchy poison ivy. But there was something else. Something Benny saw during the day wasn't quite right. What was it? He closed his eyes. He thought of the picture puzzles he loved to solve. This time he pictured the two old photos of the Applewood Café—the one he saw in Sally's real estate office and the one hanging in the Applewood Café. The photos were almost exactly the same. *Almost.*

Benny squeezed his eyes tight, trying to picture the differences. There was something else. Benny was sure of it. He just couldn't see it. Tomorrow he'd put the two photos side by side and figure out what it was.

Watch jumped on the bed and curled up next to him. "You smell like shampoo," said Benny. He slid an arm around his furry friend, and soon they fell fast asleep.

CHAPTER 7

Picture, Picture, on the Wall

After breakfast the next morning, Henry lifted one photo off the Applewood Café wall. He set it on the table next to the photo Sally gave them. Benny was right about two differences between the pictures. Only one photo had a SOLD sticker on the For Sale sign. And then Laura and David were only in one photo.

"I was sure there was something else," Benny said. But, as hard as he looked, he couldn't find any more differences.

While the others went out to work in the garden, Violet walked around the café taping up photos of Duffy's Garage. An elderly man walked in with a young woman. Violet knew who the man was. It was Cesar Canton, the old farmer who played chess with Chief Morgan.

He introduced the woman. "This is my daughter," he told Violet. "She's the one who likes living in the sky."

The woman smiled. "I'm pleased to meet a friend of Chief Morgan's. My dad was lonely and bored here in Greenfield until he and the chief began playing chess every day."

Cesar rested a hand on his daughter's shoulder as they walked to a table. Violet noticed that small blisters covered his hand. The she glanced at his cane. Could the tip of Cesar's cane have made the holes they'd found all around the garden? A shiver ran through her. She hurried out to the others and told them about Cesar's rash and his cane.

"But Cesar loves growing things," said

Jessie. "Why would he dump out our worms or dig up our plants?"

"Someone dug up my onions!" wailed Benny from the back of the garden. This time, the person didn't bother putting the plants back in place. They'd dug deep holes all around the onion patch and left the onions strewn on the ground. The heat of the morning sun had shriveled the leaves. "They're ruined," cried Benny.

"It's just the leaves that dried out," said Violet, "the onions are still good." She gathered the onions, gently setting them in a basket. "I'll bring these to Mr. Shea and he'll cook them into a delicious soup."

Benny didn't hear her. He was staring hard at Duffy's Garage next door. His eyes grew wide. "That's it!" he yelled, forgetting all about the onions. "*That's* what's different!" He ran inside and returned waving the For Sale photo of Duffy's Garage. "See? The metal sheets used to cover the *outside* of the windows." He pointed to the garage. "But now they are *inside* the windows."

The children raced over, pressing their noses against the garage windows. The sheets of metal blocked them from seeing inside. "Green paint," said Henry, pointing to drips on the metal. "That's the color of the writing on the AAA Armored Cars."

"We need to get inside," said Jessie. She ran to the café and got the key Sally had given them. It barely fit into the rusty lock. Henry jiggled it this way and that. Suddenly, the key turned and the door creaked open. The children walked inside.

The dark garage smelled like motor oil and damp cement. Violet clicked the light switch up and down. Nothing happened. The only light came from the open door.

"Stand here," said Henry. He waited for his eyes to adjust to the dark. Then he found a hammer on the tool bench and went to a window. Carefully, he slid the end of the hammer under the nails, prying off the metal panel. As he pried off the last nail, the panel clattered to the ground. Sunlight streamed in. The others rushed in, staring at the panel on the floor. It said, "AAA Armored Car Company."

"This was the thief's hideout," said Benny.

Jessie nodded. "I think the thief was the man in the ponytail. The man who rented the garage from Sally. He pulled the metal sheets off the windows and nailed them around his truck to make it look like an armored car."

Violet frowned at the green lettering, which was full of drips and smudges. "He did a messy job," she said. "Why didn't anybody notice?"

"Everyone in town was watching the circus parade," Henry reminded her.

"And our mail truck drives down our block every day," said Jessie. "When was the last time you took a good hard look at it?"

Violet tried to remember, but she couldn't. "Exactly," Jessie said. "All the crook needed to do was make his fake truck look *sort* of like the real one."

"He was pretty smart," said Henry. "After the robbery, he came back here, pulled the panels off, and nailed them back up on the windows. He hid the evidence in plain sight. I wonder what he did with the van."

Benny looked out the window at the back lot. "That used to be full of junk cars," he said. "What if the crook just parked his van with all the others?"

Jessie clapped her hands. "Benny, that's brilliant! No one would notice one more old car."

"Sam's Scrap Yard hauled the junk off Duffy's lot," said Henry, racing to his bike. "If Benny's right, maybe the van is still at Sam's."

CHAPTER 8

Black Gold Thief

The sign for Sam's Scrap Yard stuck out of a tall dirt hill. Wild leafy vines crawled along the dirt and snaked around the sign. A tangle of watermelons, cantaloupes, pumpkins, cucumbers, and zucchinis covered the hill.

The children rode their bikes past the hill into the scrap yard. There were old cars everywhere. Most were missing windows and tires. Some had no doors, others no bumpers. Many seemed more rust than paint.

"*Woof! Woof!*" A large dog came from around an old school bus.

"Cat!" called a deep voice. "Stay!" The dog stopped. A man hurried around the bus and stood next to the dog. He looked a bit like Spooky the Scarecrow with his baggy pants and rumpled shirt.

"Your dog's name is *Cat?*" Jessie asked the man.

"Yup. Already got a dog named Dog. Cat likes to bark, which makes him a good watchdog. But he wouldn't hurt a flea. Anyway, I'm Sam. Can I help you?"

Jessie handed Sam one of Duffy's *For Sale* photos. "Do you remember this place?" she asked.

"Yup, I cleared every bit of that junk." Sam squinted at the photo. "This doesn't show that old van I had to haul."

"A van?" Jessie said. Her heart beat faster. Had they found the fake armored car? "Is it still here?" she asked.

Sam scratched his stubbly beard. "Should be around someplace. Let's take a look." He led them around cars and trucks, through mountains of rusty fences and metal beams.

As they walked, Violet asked him about the vegetables growing out front.

"That's the darndest thing," said Sam. "Those hills were always an eyesore—full of weeds and all sorts of litter. But this spring, little plants came sprouting up. Every morning I came to work and found more and more plants. I figured the wind blew in a bunch of old seeds." He laughed. "I sure do like the look of all that greenery." Suddenly, Sam stopped. "There," he said, "there she is."

The van was a sorry sight. The metal trim was ripped off the sides. Gone were the tires and doors, bumpers and hood.

"What happened to it?" Henry asked.

"People come here looking for parts to fix their cars," explained Sam. "They'll take a mirror from one car and a door handle from another."

Henry examined small holes poked everywhere on the outside of the van. "Nail holes," he said. "The thief hammered the metal panels right into the sides of this van."

Violet peered inside. "There's green paint on the steering wheel," she said. "The thief touched it while he was painting." She looked closely at the paint. "I think I see finger-prints!"

Jessie examined the back of the driver's seat. The plastic headrest was torn. Pieces of yellow foam crumbled out. A few long blond hairs were caught in the jagged plastic. She remembered what Sally had said, that the man who rented Duffy's Garage had a long blond ponytail. Jessie touched the strands.

"These aren't real hair. That ponytail was a wig. And these," she touched a couple of black hairs caught in the torn leather, "might be hairs from the black wig he wore when he robbed the bank." She started to pull the hairs out.

"Stop!" warned Henry. "We mustn't touch any of this. It's all evidence." He read detective books and he knew that it was best not to touch anything that the police might need to solve a case. He saw that the floor of the van was littered with old newspapers, paint rags, fast food, and candy wrappers. Henry wanted to climb in and look through everything. But he knew he couldn't. "Let's go," he said. "We have to tell the police what we've found."

* * * *

Chief Morgan sat at the front desk typing up a police report. Next to him was a a plate of cookies, with a sign that said: *Fresh baked zucchini cookies—help yourself.*

"We found it!" cried Benny. "We found the fake armored car!"

In a rush, the Aldens told the chief about everything they'd found—the van and the metal panels nailed on to make it look like an armored car, the stranger with the blond ponytail who'd rented Duffy's Garage . . .

As they talked, the chief waved over two detectives who wrote down the children's information. One of them hurried off to Sam's Scrap Yard while the other went to Duffy's Garage.

"Should we wait here," asked Jessie, "in case the detectives have questions for us?"

"They won't be back for a while," said the chief. "I'll call your house when I learn anything. Meanwhile, take a few cookies with you." He pushed the plate toward them. "My wife's been baking zucchini cookies, zucchini cakes, zucchini sweet rolls— you name it, she bakes it. Zucchini is growing wild all over town. Watermelons, too, and cantaloupes, cucumbers, tomatoes."

Violet nibbled a cookie thick with raisins. "We saw your friend Cesar Canton and his daughter at the Applewood Café," she said. "His daughter says he misses his farm. She is very happy you and Cesar play chess every day."

"Not every day," said the Chief. "We just play Saturday and Sunday." He emptied the rest of the cookies into a bag. "Here, take them all. If I eat one more cookie, I'll turn into a zucchini."

As the children unlocked their bikes, Jessie said, "The chief said he plays chess with

Cesar twice a week. But Cesar's daughter *thinks* Cesar is playing chess every day." She smiled. "What do you think Cesar is doing the *other* five days of the week?"

All around them, vegetables grew around lampposts and parking meters and trees and fences. "I think Cesar does what he loves to do most," said Violet. "Planting, planting, planting."

"Did he plant the hill around Sam's Scrap Yard?" asked Benny. "And the tomatoes outside the wig shop?"

Violet nodded. "He's planted this whole town."

"I'll bet Cesar staked our sunflowers," Jessie said. "And he got poison ivy on his hands when he cleaned up those weeds behind the Applewood Café."

Violet looked troubled. "His daughter said farming is too hard for him. Do you think we should tell her what he's been doing?"

The children didn't want Cesar to hurt himself by working too hard. But they also did not want to give away the old farmer's secret. "Let's ask Grandfather tonight," said Jessie. "He'll know the right thing to do. And he will keep Cesar's secret."

* * * *

They biked through the park, where the Heart Healthy Run had been the day before. The yellow-shirted Events Committee members were working to take down the tents. Empty water bottles littered the finish line.

The man with the metal detector was there, too, searching the ground nearby.

"Hi," Benny called. The man looked up, startled. "I tried one of those," Benny told him. "I heard the clicking sounds that metal makes and—"

But the man did not want to talk. He hurried away, kicking aside water bottles, stomping over cardboard signs.

Violet stared at the man's boot prints. They left a *V* shaped pattern. One of the Vs had no point on the bottom. "That's the same boot print we saw in our garden," she said. "That's the man who dumped our worms."

The man was running now. "Hey," yelled Henry. The man ran faster. "We want to talk to you!"

They started to ride after him.

But suddenly, a scream stopped them cold. "Look out!" cried a voice across the park.

The children turned to look. The top of a big tent rocked back and forth. The sides started falling in. The volunteers were inside! The children raced over and jumped off their bikes.

Henry grabbed one of the tent poles. "Jessie, grab another pole," he called. Benny and Violet helped, too. Together they held the tent steady enough for the trapped workers to escape.

"Thank you," said a man. "We...we thought we could take the tents down by ourselves. But we really needed one more worker."

"It's just like Fenster to disappear when there's hard work to be done," said an angry woman. "Why did he volunteer for the Events Committee? He knew we needed his help with the tents."

"We'll help," said the children. And, with everyone working together, they took down all the tents and packed them away. By the time they finished, the man with the metal detector was gone.

"That's all right," said Henry, "I have an idea how we can track him down. Let's go to Mr. Hamu's hardware store."

At the hardware store, Mr. Hamu switched on his computer. "I hope I can help you find the person who has been trespassing in your garden," he told the Aldens. "Only a few people have bought this expensive kind of metal detector." He typed the words *Metal Detector Model X332* in the computer. Three names appeared on the screen.

He pointed to the first name. "This man moved to Chicago last year," he said. He pointed to another name. "And this man fell off his son's skateboard and broke his leg, so he's not using his detector just now. That leaves this last one. His name is Chaney Dunkard. He lives just down the street." Mr. Hamu wrote down the address.

"Thank you, Mr. Hamu," said Jessie. "We'll talk to him." She and the other Aldens hoped they could find out who had been making trouble in their garden.

The children biked up to the small house. They saw Mr. Dunkard working at a picnic table in his front yard. He sorted through a pile of metal objects. Jewelry went in one green cloth bag and coins in another. When he saw the children, his eyes bugged out. "What do you want?"

"Why did you dump out our black gold?" Benny demanded.

The man snorted. "You mean that heap of wormy dirt?'"

Benny jutted out his chin. "Worm poop is black gold."

"Worm poop!" Mr. Dunkard made a face. "Yuck!"

"Why did you dump it?" Benny asked again.

"I heard you talking in the café about 'black gold.' I thought you meant real gold. You said it was in garbage cans," the man answered.

"The cans were on the Applewood Café property," said Jessie. "At least you could have cleaned up the mess you made."

"I heard someone coming," said the man, "so I left. Big deal."

"Why did you dig up Benny's tomato plants?" asked Violet. "And his peppers and his onions?"

"I don't know what you're talking about," Mr. Dunkard said "I didn't dig up anything. I may have snooped around in some cans, but I don't dig in other people's yards."

"Hey, look!" Benny said. He picked up one of the green cloth bags on the table. "This is the same kind of bag we used to make Spooky's head!"

Mr. Dunkard yanked the bags back. "These are mine. I found them in the alley behind the Applewood Café. They were in the *alley* garbage can, *not* on Applewood property. Finders keepers."

"May I see them?" asked Henry.

"No. You can get out of my yard, is what

you can do." The man with went back to sorting through the treasures he had found. "Worm poop," he muttered. "Who calls worms 'black gold?' Kids. Bah."

As the Aldens got back on their bikes, they were all thinking the same thing. If Mr. Dunkard didn't dig up the "traveling tomatoes," then who did?

CHAPTER 9

Hot, Hotter, Hottest

The children stopped back at the police station on their way home.

"The detective brought back the metal panels from Duffy's Garage," the chief said. "Those will make great evidence once we dust them for fingerprints. No word yet from the other detective about the van. I promise I'll call as soon as I hear."

None of the children liked waiting. It was always more fun to be doing something than doing nothing. But as they walked outside, they couldn't think of what to do next.

"Well," said Violet, "we did solve two mysteries. We know it was Cesar who propped up our sunflowers and cleared the poison ivy out of the alley. And we also know that Mr. Dunkard dumped our compost cans searching for 'black gold.'"

Henry laughed. "I wish I could have seen his face when all he found was garbage and a million worms. But someone else dug around our garden, and we don't know why. We need to think harder."

"I want to keep trying to find the bank robber," said Jessie. She sat on the police department steps. "But I'm out of ideas."

"Me, too," said Violet, joining her.

"Me, three," said Benny, plopping down between them.

But Henry was not ready to give up. "Look, we've learned important things. We know the thief hid his van in Duffy's Garage while he made it into an armored car. Then we found the van. We just don't know who the thief is."

Jessie twirled a lock of her hair. She thought about the van in the scrap yard . She twirled and twirled her . . . hair! "Wigs!" she cried, jumping up. "The thief wore wigs!"

"So?" said Benny.

But Jessie was already running down the block. "And he wore a uniform," she called to the others. "He wore wigs and a uniform. But we didn't see wigs or a uniform in Duffy's Garage or in the van."

Suddenly, her feet flew out from under her. Her right leg went east and her left leg went west. She landed with a thud. "I'm okay, I'm okay," she called, getting up. She'd slipped on some tomatoes!

"They're Cesar's tomatoes," said Benny. It was true. Ripe tomatoes littered the ground. They fell from the plants growing all down the block.

"Come on!" yelled Jessie, waving to the others as she disappeared inside Cora's Costumes.

This time, Cora was dressed like a rock star in a sparkly sequin dress and a spiky wig.

Jessie told her what they were looking for. "We need to look up someone who rented two wigs," she said.

"Two wigs," Cora repeated. She typed *wigs* into her computer. A list came up. She clicked on *Cheerleader.* "That's what I call our pony-tail wig," she explained. She printed out all the names of people who had rented a cheer-leader wig in the past two months. Then she typed *Elvis wig* into the computer. "That's our black wig with sideburns," she said. She printed out another list of names. The children compared the two lists. One name appeared on both.

"Mr. Malfrat rented both wigs the same day," said Jessie. "Did he rent anything else?"

Cora typed *Malfrat* into the computer. "Yes, here, Mr. Malfrat, size large, rented two wigs and a blue policeman's uniform for four days." The date of his order was two days before the robbery. "We were so busy with the circus costumes that I honestly can't remember a thing about him. Wait, what's this?" She scrolled down the screen. "Ah, here. I made a note that after he returned the costume I had to repair the police patch on the sleeve. It looked like it came off and someone tried to sew it back on. Hold on, I'll get it for you."

Cora returned carrying the uniform. It was the same blue as the AAA Armored Car driver's uniform. Violet ran her hand over the police patch on the sleeve. "The thief could have clipped this off, robbed the bank, then sewed it back before returning the costume."

Henry borrowed Cora's computer to search the Greenfield phone directory.

"There's no Mr. Malfrat listed," he said. "And the address is fake."

"Another dead end," said Jessie.

The Aldens left the costume store and walked down the block, careful to step around the squished tomatoes that littered the sidewalk. Looking at the tomatoes made Benny hungry. But he didn't want a tomato. He wanted something sweet. He was about to ask if they could stop for ice cream when Violet spoke up.

"Why would a bank robber return the rented uniform and wigs?" Violet asked. "Why not just steal those, too? He could have thrown them into the river or buried them or burned them. But he returned them."

"I think this proves that the thief lives right here in town!" Henry said.

"It does?" asked Jessie.

"Sure," said Henry. "If he'd left town after the robbery, he wouldn't care what happened to the uniform and wigs. But if he was here in Greenfield, he couldn't risk making Cora suspicious. She might connect the missing rented uniform with the uniform worn at the robbery."

Benny was tired of talking about costumes. "Could we get ice cream?" he asked.

"We'll stop at the ice cream parlor," said Jessie.

Benny pulled a crumpled dollar bill out of his pocket. "Wait, I don't have enough money," he said sadly.

"Well," said Jessie, "it might not be enough for an ice cream. But it's more than enough for a vending machine. Let's go to that one we saw at the bank"

At the bank, Benny studied the goodies in the vending machine window. So many wonderful choices! Should he buy cookies, something salty, or something chewy? As he tried to decide, the vending machine man came and began refilling the machine.

"That's the one!" cried Benny as the man refilled the last row with red-wrapped candy bars. "That's the one I want to try."

"You sure?" asked the man, closing the door.

"Yup," said Benny. He fed his dollar into the machine and pressed C-5. Out came a Chili-Billy Bar. Benny tore off the wrapper and took a big bite. He chewed and chewed, waiting for the sweet candy to fill his mouth. He stopped chewing. His eyes grew wide. Wider. "Oh," he said. "Ohhhhhh." The candy was spicy *hot!*

He ran to the drinking fountain. For a

long time he stood there, letting the water cool his tongue. "Yuck!" he said at last.

Violet picked up the red Chili-Billy bar Benny dropped. She recognized it at once. "This is the same red wrapper Fenster threw on the ground at the park," she said.

"That candy is hard to find," said the vending machine man. "Most places don't carry it. Last week, some guy bought my entire supply. He was going on a trip and wanted to take some with him."

* * * *

Benny still had the yucky taste in his mouth when the children stopped at the police station. They told Chief Morgan about the wigs and uniform rented by a Mr. Malfrat. "Malfrat?" said the chief. His thick eyebrows came together. "That's an interesting name. French, I think."

"May I please have some water?" asked Benny.

Chief Morgan brought him a nice big cup. "Here you go, Benny." He looked at the

others. "Anyone else need some watering?"

"Watering?" gasped Jessie. "Oh my gosh! This is Tuesday. This is the day we water the garden."

Watering was one of the most important garden chores. It was also the most fun. And the work would keep the children busy. Maybe, by the time they finished, they'd find out what the detectives had found in the robber's van.

CHAPTER 10

The Scarecrow's Surprise

The Aldens finished watering the plants and turned off their hoses. Mrs. Shea carried a pitcher of lemonade out to the garden. The children joined her and the twins in the shade of a large oak tree. Henry leaned back on his elbows and looked at their garden. Spooky the Scarecrow smiled his crooked smile.

"What do you use those green bags for?" asked Henry.

"Green bags?" said Mrs. Shea.

Henry pointed at the scarecrow. "Like the one we used to make Spooky's head."

"I thought you found that bag in the alley," said Mrs. Shea.

"We did," Benny explained. "But the metal detector man had bags just like that. He found them in your garbage cans, too."

Mrs. Shea shrugged. "David and I don't use them. I have no idea where they're from." The twins began fussing, and she took them inside for their naps.

Henry went over and walked slowly around the scarecrow, staring at its head. Suddenly, he reached up and ripped the head right off Spooky's body.

"Henry!" cried Violet. "I worked hard stitching that head to Grandfather's shirt."

"Sorry," said Henry, bringing them the scarecrow head. He set it on the ground. "Don't these look like letters?" asked Henry.

Behind the mouth and eyes that Benny had drawn, they could make out faint letters:

r enf eld B n

Violet ran to her bike bag and brought back a black marker. The others watched as the young artist slowly traced over the letters. Then she filled in the faded letters:

Greenfield Bank

"This is the bank's money bag!" said Jessie. "The thief must have buried the money right here after the robbery."

Benny jumped up. "We've been gardening on top of bags of stolen money?"

"That's explains why your tomatoes were moving," said Henry. "The thief hid the money under our plants. Then he dug them up when he needed the money. He put your plants back so no one would know."

"*I* knew," said Benny.

Henry smiled. "That's because you kept a measuring chart."

Violet capped her pen. "After he dug up a bag, the thief took the cash out and tossed the bag into the garbage."

"Why didn't he take *all* the money with him after the robbery?" asked Jessie. "Why did he hide it here and just dig up a little at a time?"

"Maybe it's like our bank accounts," said Benny. "We put our money in the bank to keep it safe until there's something special we want to buy."

Jessie hugged her little brother. "Benny, you're a genius! That's exactly what our garden is. It's the robber's bank! For some reason, he can't take the loot home."

Benny laughed. "Maybe he's afraid someone will steal it. Get it? Steal from the stealer?"

"Or," said Henry, a knowing smile on his lips, "maybe he's afraid someone will *find* it. Maybe he lives with someone who is very nosey. Someone who goes through his drawers and his closet and—"

"Fenster!" the others shouted.

"He is big," said Benny, "like the thief."

"And he seems too lazy to work," said Jessie, "but he has money to buy expensive watches."

"You're wrong," said Violet. "It can't be him. Remember, we saw his photo in the newspaper. The day of the robbery, Fenster was at the circus train with the other Special Events Committee members. It was noon on the city hall clock."

"That was at the *beginning* of the parade," said Henry. "The robbery was twenty minutes later. Fenster could have left right after the picture was taken. He could have robbed the bank."

"I'm not sure," said Violet. "He would have to rob the bank, drive back to Duffy's, tear the panels off his van, and nail them up on the windows. Then he would have to bury the money in our garden. And he'd have to do all that and still make it back to the park by the time the March of the Elephants got there."

"Maybe he didn't make it back in time," said Jessie. "Does anyone remember seeing Fenster's picture at the end of the parade?" No one did.

"We need to look at those newspaper photos again," said Violet. "Let's go back to the library."

* * * *

The Aldens spread the newspapers out on a library table and studied the pictures in the special circus section.

"Look for the people in the yellow shirts," Jessie said. "Let's see if Fenster's with them."

"Here's a photo taken at noon," said Violet. "I can see the City Hall clock in the background!" In the photo, five people in yellow shirts greeted the circus parade. Fenster stood right in front, grinning at the camera.

"But I can't find him in any of the photos taken later on, in the park," Jessie pointed out. In those pictures, the children could find only four people in yellow shirts.

"I think Fenster is using the circus as his alibi," said Henry. "He made sure the newspaper photographer took his picture. If people think he was at the circus all day, then they won't think he robbed the bank."

"But can we prove that he wasn't at the circus later?" asked Jessie. "He wasn't in the other photos, but the police will need more proof than that."

"What about the day of the 5K race?" asked Violet. "The Events Committee was in charge of that. Everyone in town was there, including the Sheas. Was Fenster at the race, or was he at the Applewood Café digging up money he hid under Benny's green peppers?"

The children clicked to the *Greenfield Gazette* website and typed *5K race*. Hundreds of photos were posted. They couldn't find Fenster in any of them. "This still isn't real proof," said Jessie.

The children grew quiet. It wasn't enough to suspect someone. Maybe the detectives would find Fenster's fingerprints in the van.

"Oh, dear," said Violet. "What if he's getting ready to make his getaway?"

"What makes you think that?" Henry asked.

"Benny's onions," said Violet. "They were dug up, just like the tomatoes and peppers. But the onions were left scattered all around. At first, Fenster was trying to put things back, and hide the fact that he was digging up the garden. But now he doesn't care . . . because he's taking off."

"He wasn't at the park to help his committee take down the tents," agreed Jessie.

"And he talked about France," said Benny. "How he liked French restaurants."

"Fenster bought that watch with two faces," said Henry. "The one he could set for Greenfield and for Paris."

"And the vending machine man said someone bought all the Chili-Billy Bars," said Benny. "Someone going on a trip."

"Do you think he's already escaped?" asked Violet.

Henry looked at his watch. It was nearly three. "Mr. Witlin told Fenster to pick up his new watch at three o'clock today. Maybe it's not too late. Maybe we can still stop him!"

As they rushed out, Violet told the librarian to call the police. "Tell them to go to Witlin's Watch Works on Main Street."

"And," shouted Benny, running after the others, "tell them to *hurry!*"

* * * *

The children's hearts pounded as they pulled up alongside Witlin's Watch Works. Careful to stay out of view, they climbed off their bikes and quietly leaned them against the jungle of tomatoes growing on the side of the shop. They peeked into the store window. Fenster stood at the counter. "He's trying on his new watch," whispered Jessie.

"He's all dressed up," said Violet, "the way Grandfather dresses when he's going on a trip."

"We have to stall him until the police arrive," Henry said.

Jessie noticed a taxi waiting at the curb. She noticed the splattered tomatoes all along the sidewalk. She had an idea.

She ran around to the driver's side. "Are you waiting for a big man in the watch shop?" she asked the driver.

"Yup," the cabbie said.

"Are you taking him to the airport?"

"Yup. His suitcases are in the trunk," the cabbie replied.

"Well," Jessie said, "if you bring those

suitcases to the police station right now, you will receive a very large reward. A reward for helping lead to the arrest of a bank robber."

The taxi driver peered at Jessie and then at the other children. "You're James Alden's grandchildren, aren't you?"

"We are," said Jessie.

"Well, there's not a more honest man in town," he said. "I reckon you are every bit as honest as your grandfather." He held up his cell phone. "Want me to call the police?"

"They're already on their way," said Jessie. "But, if you really want to help, please start your car and pull away. And honk your horn nice and loud."

"Will do." The man started the taxi and, as he drove off, honked his horn over and over.

Just as Jessie hoped, Fenster heard the honking. He raced to the window in time to see the taxi driving away. "Wait," he shouted, running out of the store. "My suitcases. Stop! Come back! Come—"

His fancy dress shoes hit the slippery tomatoes. His feet flew into the air. "Yikes!"

he shouted, as he landed with a crash. Fenster tried to stand but his feet flew out again. Finally, Fenster got on his hands and knees and began to crawl away. But by then, the sound of sirens filled the air as police cars squealed around the corner and screeched to a stop.

"Careful of the tomatoes," warned Benny. The police handcuffed Fenster and led him to the squad car.

As he climbed in, Fenster glowered at the children. "This is all your fault," he snarled. "Who gave me away?"

"You can blame it on the scarecrow," said Benny. But he didn't think Fenster heard.

The Sheas threw a celebration at the Applewood Café to thank the children for finding the robber. "I remembered why the name Malfrat was so familiar," said Chief Morgan. "You said Fenster rented the wigs and police uniform using the name Malfrat. Well, Malfrat isn't a person. Malfrat is the French word for 'crook.'"

Mr. Shea baked a tall cake in the shape of

the Greenfield Bank. The icing said: HOORAY FOR OUR HEROES.

"We couldn't have done it without Cesar's tomatoes," said Benny, eating a corner piece with lots of icing.

Jessie carried in an armful of tomatoes. "We just picked these from around the neighborhood," she said. "Help yourselves!"

Cesar's daughter stood and clapped her hands. "I have an announcement," she said. "Thanks to all of you, I've learned how much it means to my father to grow things. Today, I bought Duffy's Garage. I will help my father turn it into a greenhouse. Now he can grow plants all year around."

Everyone cheered.

"Well," said Benny, "you'd better plant plenty of tomatoes. You just never know when another bank robber might come along!"